Portal

And Other Tales

ROLAND McELROY

DEDICATION

For her support when I am hesitating,
For her inspiration when ideas cease to flow,
For her encouragement when I am tempted to doubt,
For her creative skill with images, graphics, layouts and proofing,
This book is dedicated to my dear wife, Bettie,
Without whom the moving finger would not write at all.

CONTENTS

INTRODUCTION

I t is not easy to see light when almost everyone else sees darkness. Very few possess that gift—and make no mistake, it is a gift. Fewer still are the number of people who can see within the light an open door that leads to the wonderment of our future— the inventions, innovations, discoveries—so easy to dismiss today as simply figments of human imaginations.

There was a time in the not so distant past when no one would have believed the human voice could be carried by a copper wire to the ear of a friend hundreds of miles away, or a time when moving images would be transmitted around the world via satellites stationed in synchronous orbits above Earth. A visit by humans to Mars is not dismissed any more as unachievable.

Most of the major scientific advancements that have changed the course of our history and opened new worlds to us, came from harnessing the invisible potential of an element or an electron. Movement of air has already been harnessed by the military to knock a man off his feet. Why not increase the energy and lift a five-ton rock off the ground in order to move the levitated rock with ease to another location. Why not add vibration to the mix and combine the frequency of Earth's naturally occurring rate of vibration with Earth's magnetic field, thus, to create a force powerful enough to open an energy portal from which humans could be transported to another dimension.

Nikola Tesla created a schematic for generating alternating current from an image that came to him in a dream. What marvelous ideas are in the incubation stage right now, just waiting to interrupt someone's dream?

With open minds, and the generous sharing of knowledge with our human companions on Earth, I am optimistic that together we will innovate in every aspect of our existence to avoid destruction of our Earth, strengthen our stewardship of its resources, and prepare us for a time when we will step into the wonderment of the Universe.

Welcome, open minds, to *Portal.*

Following *Portal*, three short stories are included, each inspired by the author's compelling drive to write something new every day.

The first, *Cocoon*, an episodic memoir, is drawn from the author's early struggle to come of age in a small Southern town which seemed stuck in the middle of the 19th century.

The fictional story, *Crossroads*, was captured by the author one morning on an almost clean napkin while he was enjoying his favorite dark roast coffee at The Last Drop café surrounded by friends and at least one Russian spy who shared his addiction to caffeine.

Another episodic memoir, *Six, At Last*, originates from a series of strictly haphazard events that stick like a fly in the spider web memory of the author's first six years.

Roland McElroy

PORTAL

A Step Too Far

"If you want to find the secrets of the universe, think in terms of energy, frequency and vibration."
--Nikola Tesla

Wire Copy

Reuters - July 1, 2024, Sedona, AZ

10:30 PM EST
Updated 3 minutes ago

Astrophysicist escapes serious injury conducting Cathedral Rock experiment

Dr. Adele Abramson, professor of astrophysics at Arizona State University, has theorized that Sedona's Cathedral Rock possesses the strongest energy vortex in Arizona, and "if stimulated properly, will open a portal to higher dimensions or perhaps a wormhole to the other side of the universe."

Reputable astrophysicists have frequently dismissed her experiments as "pure fantasy."

Whatever the nature of her recent experiment at Cathedral Rock, the result was a serious third degree burn on one hip. Park rangers took her to a local emergency room where she waved off treatment and refused to stay overnight for observation. The source of the injury was not disclosed.

A colleague at Arizona State believes Dr. Abramson hopes to harness the Earth's magnetic field for her experiments in inter-dimensional travel. "Others have tried," said Physics Department head, Dr. William Sears, "but no one has succeeded."

—staff writer, Alex Whitener

Coffee in Giza

The Associated Press offered an assignment to the Middle East beat three years ago, and I believed it would get me out of that burbling cauldron of political intrigue in Washington. I snatched it up. I've had no visitors from the states, and none expected until yesterday when I received a text from my ages-ago friend, Dr. Adele Abramson. Of all the people from my past who might contact me in Egypt, she would be the last on my list. We shared little in common, and our paths seldom crossed. Indeed, high School years were the last time we were face-to-face. And—I'll just say it—I was crazy about her. She had no interest in me. The last I heard she was teaching astrophysics at Arizona State. Now she's here and anxious to meet.

"Let's have coffee," she texted, "just two old friends catching up on their lives." Old friends, yes, lovers, no—although I tried. God knows I tried.

Now, she wants to have coffee? Really? Her text sounded a bit insincere. Of course, that could be a hardened cynical interpretation from one who was rejected too many times to count.

In the distance, an Egyptian nightjar calls to its mate. *Kind of a lonely sound. Maybe that's why the old folks believe the sight of one is a harbinger of doom . . . or maybe the nightjar is just looking for an evening meal.*

She wants something from me. What . . . and why? All right, let's get it over with.

About a mile from Khufu's pyramid in Giza, there's a little coffee house—Cilantro Café—the perfect spot for a rendezvous of any kind—romantic or otherwise. We agreed to meet at 8 o'clock, but that was ten minutes ago. I'm already sensing this rendezvous will fall into the category of "otherwise."

When tourists stumble into the Cilantro, they're usually completely lost or looking for an American burger and Coke. Egyptians, however, and at least one American reporter, come here for the strong Ethiopian coffee.

Hmmm . . . not too many tourists tonight. The air is nearly unbreathable, saturated as it is with the heady aroma of strong Yirgachefe coffee and the acrid smell of cheap Egyptian cigars.

An unblended dark roast from anywhere is welcome in my mug any time of day. Tonight's coffee, however, has an earthy taste like a gritty mixture of Molokhia soup and overcooked spinach. I'll give it one thing; it does have body, and I'll drink almost anything if it affords me an opportunity to spend time with Adele Abramson. She has a hold on my affection that—I confess—to this day has not diminished one iota.

I've been waiting for Adele since fifth grade. And it always ends the same way. A solitary person—me—sitting alone in a back booth. She doesn't know that . . .

James Maloney, don't go there. Don't even think about it.

Adele was the smartest student in my high school physics class, maybe the smartest in our entire school. Every teacher loved her, and of course, so did every teenage boy, every lusting one of them. And with the unblemished complexion of a Chinese porcelain doll, she was the envy of every girl. No acne or any other puberty induced imperfections. Just the natural beauty of perfect skin, long shapely legs on an hourglass perfect body, blue eyes, of course, and a crown of shoulder length blonde hair that displayed a flippant curl and an attitude that said, "yes, I know I'm gorgeous." I asked her out at least a hundred times, but she always had her eye on a football player or that guy who had the mysterious quality of being from "out of town." She was never available for me, not even for one date. I don't count that back booth incident that occurred in the middle of a random afternoon.

DO NOT go there. Where IS she now?

When we became seniors, the pool of available males diminished for senior girls, creating a crisis for many. No problem for Adele. By the time we rose to senior status, her eyes were already focused on "college men." Every girl, it seemed, wanted to date one of those sophisticated and mature scholars of nineteen years.

And so, I waited, and I guess I'm still waiting . . . at the Cilantro Café in Giza.

The reporter in me says, get up and leave right now, but the hopelessly in love fool in me says maybe she really is interested. On the other hand, what could I possibly do for Adele now—twenty years since college, twenty years of following different paths? Of course, what could she ask of me that I wouldn't do?

Yes, I know this is not going to end well . . . but . . . maybe . . . maybe I should wait a little longer.

In the darkness of the dimly lit café, the familiar fragrance of Chanel No.5 broke through the repulsive blend of cigar smoke and dark roast coffee, and a second later, that mellifluous voice that held me enthralled so many years ago shut out all others in the room.

"Hello, James. It's great to see you."

She still has the softest voice I've ever heard—soft, and yet, firm, if that's possible. To my ears, the sound of her speaking conveys an overwhelming sense of authority, and yes, even emotional intimacy—if that's possible.

Adele leaned in and gave my cheek a little peck in the same way she might greet a third cousin she'd met only once. Just a little peck. Like a second cousin, maybe.

"Great to see you, too, Adele. You haven't changed a bit."

'Fools rush in where wise men fear to tread.' Why does that old Platters song play in my brain?

"James, do you know the summer solstice is tomorrow?"

What kind of conversation is this? Two old friends meet again after many years apart, and she wants to talk about the solstice.

She didn't wait for me to answer. Instead, she placed a small match box in my hand, leaned closer and whispered, "You're holding the key to unlocking the universe. This little thing will light a fire hotter than any match you've ever held."

But not as hot as a kiss from you—a kiss that, undoubtedly, I will never know.

"How's your coffee, Adele? Mine could use another shot of espresso. Are the Egyptians aware there is better coffee roasted in Ethiopia, even Kenya . . .?"

Adele's palm slapped the table. "Forget the coffee, James." Two tourists at a nearby table hurriedly got up and left. Her voice was no longer soft. "Listen to me."

I've heard that impatient, no nonsense tone before.

"All things vibrate. You and I vibrate.

I know I'm vibrating now.

"Our internal organs vibrate—the heart and brain vibrate. Even Earth vibrates."

"Seriously?

"Of course. Earth vibrates at a rate of 7.83 Hertz—its resonant frequency. To put it in layman's terms, that's the frequency of Earth's vibration when it is in tune with all of nature. All matter has a vibrating rate. Back in the '50s, a German scientist—Schumann, I believe—spent a year measuring global electromagnetic resonances in the extremely low frequency range and determined the resonant frequency of Earth."

"But 7.83 Hertz? Isn't that below the range of human hearing?"

"Yes, of course."

"Then, what good is it?"

"Look, Jack . . ."

She always called me by the first name that popped into her head when she was irritated and impatient. Jack, I suppose, is better than Herman.

"Sound—perhaps I should explain it this way—the movement of air produces sound, including sounds inaudible to you and me; they're either too low or too high. You've heard about elephants bellowing loud enough to wake the dead?

I nodded even though I hadn't heard.

"Well, it might surprise you to know they also use vibrations transmitted silently through the Earth's crust to communicate with each other over long distances. The sounds elephants produce via vibrations can range from 5 Hertz to 20 Hertz."

"Why can't you and I hear those low frequency sounds?"

"Humans aren't made that way. I've been tested many times and cannot hear anything lower than 20 Hertz. Some people can hear 12 Hertz, but 7.83 Hertz—not at all."

"So, what does that have to do with this little match box I'm holding in my hand?

"It's not the box; it's the crystal inside that's part of a complex, uh, yet simple puzzle."

"Which part of the puzzle is the crystal, the complex or the simple part?"

"Both. Work with me, James. You're holding a quartz crystal with a fundamental frequency of 8.1 Hertz."

"Wait a second; what happened to 7.83 Hertz?"

"I told you it was complex; now listen to me. A frequency of 7.83 Hertz is, indeed, the heartbeat of Mother Earth. Unfortunately, it's not constant; it varies, depending on where you're standing on Earth. That's why I got burned at Cathedral Rock. You read about that?"

I nodded.

"Everything was going well—for a while. Earth's frequency was 7.83 Hertz when I measured it, but at a critical moment in my experiment, the frequency jumped above 9 Hertz, and that's when I got this."

She pulled down the waistband of her khakis, revealing a rectangular shaped scar on her hip.

"My God, that looks deep." My right hand reached out . . .

"Don't touch it!" She smacked my hand away.

That scar looks like it was made with a white hot branding iron. Must have been at least a third degree burn. Adele was always proud of her blemish free complexion but now she's eagerly showing off a scar, not a minor blemish at all but a deep and permanent scar . . . from a very hot crystal.

"You always were the one to insist on testing the heat of a stove by touching its burner." I chuckled to myself, held my mug high, and turned it upside down, nodding at the waiter. "So, Adele," I said, trying to convey an air of at least average intelligence, "what do you plan to do with this knowledge, transport yourself to another dimension?" I gave her an ever so slight smile, but she never changed her deadly serious expression.

"That *is* precisely my plan," Adele said, "and tomorrow we'll start the journey with *that* pyramid." She pointed a finger over her shoulder in the direction of the one object that towers above everything around here—the Great Pyramid of Giza. "We can talk about those higher dimensions later."

Willing my hands to stop shaking at the idea of what she was suggesting, I said, "I'd like to endorse your ambition to jump from our comfortable three dimensions into the unknown real estate of a fourth or fifth dimension, but, Adele—listen to me—it defies rational thought. In fact, it's crazy."

"It may defy *your* rational thought, my dear James, not mine!"

"My God, Adele, what prompted this insane adventure right here in the shadow of Khufu's pyramid?"

"A couple of years ago, I stood at the base of Khufu's pyramid looking up at its peak and remembered a story I was told about Sir William Siemens, a 19th century British electrical engineer who climbed to the top of the pyramid. In his day, you were free to climb to the

top any time of day if you had the stamina. And he did. When he reached the top, one of his guides challenged him to raise his hand to the sky and see what would happen. Siemens raised the index finger of his right hand, and at once felt a distinct prickling sensation. Others have had the same experience over the years. Think of it! Imagine the power that must be waiting there to be tapped?"

"And you think that power exists within the resonant frequency of Earth? Just waiting for you, Adele Abramson, to tap into it?"

"Yes, of course. And why not?"

"I didn't think you'd be so ready to become a human lightning rod. One man gets a prickling in his finger . . . "

Adele tapped her fingers impatiently. "Listen, James, it all starts with the resonant frequency of 8.1 Hertz within this pyramid, specifically the King's Chamber. Whoever designed the pyramid understood its true purpose and built it to precise specifications, including the King's Chamber which consistently resonates at 8.1 Hertz. The Giza Pyramid's stable 8.1 Hertz frequency will be the controlling factor I didn't have at Cathedral Rock."

"Wait a second. Stop. 'True purpose?' This is a tomb, right?"

"No one was ever buried here. Haven't you ever wondered why? The sarcophagus has always been empty. Because the resonant frequency of Earth varies, someone moved the sarcophagus around within the chamber to tune the room to a constant frequency of 8.1 Hertz. My 8.1 Hertz crystal will be a substitute for the large quartz crystals that once lined the walkway to the chamber. The crystal you're holding will excite remaining quartz crystals embedded in the walls at precisely 8.1 Hertz, converting the pyramid into a giant tuning fork that will use the Earth's magnetic field to multiply the energy at this specific vortex."

I gave her a confounded glance, tilted my head from side to side, and rolled my eyes.

"Sometimes Earth's frequency soars to more than 9 Hertz and suddenly drops to as low as 7.5 Hertz. It can be quite unstable as I discovered painfully at Cathedral Rock."

"But . . .this is lunacy, Adele!"

"Stay with me, James. I needed some means of holding the frequency constant at 8.1 Hertz at all the energy vortices around the globe, that is, all that are connected by the Earth's ley lines."

"Never heard of, uh, ley lines; are these ley lines invisible?"

"Of course, they're invisible. They are straight line alignments that connect all the identified energy vortices on the planet, sites where Earth's energy has been measured closest to 8.1 Hertz. Maintaining that specific frequency is critical to generating enough energy to reach another dimension."

"What happens if you aren't able to generate enough energy to reach another dimension?"

"You may get a burn like this one." Adele pulled down her waistband to show me the scar again.

I reached out, expecting to have my hand smacked, but Adele gave me a coy little smile. My shaking index finger traced the outline of her scar. This time, she didn't pull away.

The reporter in me battled my own desire to be closer to her.

"Adele, will this portal thing get you to your destination in one piece?" I tried to use my most serious tone.

"I think you understand completely what I'm up to, my dear friend."

"And this portal will bring you back?"

Adele nodded, but not convincingly.

"Do you know how crazy this idea sounds?"

"To a layperson, it may sound crazy. That's what they said about Edison's light bulb, until it worked. So was Kennedy's pledge to send a man to the moon, until it was done."

"Okay. Okay. I get your point. But how much energy is needed to open a portal?"

"I don't know. My colleagues at Cal Tech have tried to convince me that 8.1 Hertz is so low in frequency that it's likely to quickly dissipate and vanish into thin air with whatever carrier you are able to tune to an 8.1 Hertz crystal oscillator. Of course, those same colleagues dismissed FRBs, or fast radio bursts as astronomers called them when they were first heard back in 2021. FRBs have been measured at very low frequencies, frequencies that have traveled thousands of light years to reach us *without* dissipation."

"So, would it be correct to say it's about frequency *and* power?"

"Maybe."

'Maybe' is as close to correct as I've ever been.

"Will we need more than one energy vortex?"

"I don't know. There are hundreds of sites around the world that claim a special connection to a higher power."

"You think they're all legitimate?"

"I doubt it. Regardless, whether it's one, three or six energy sources, I believe they'll have to be connected in some way to increase their energy."

"Okay, Adele, let's start with the crystal. Where did you find this crystal? You didn't get it at the Apple Store."

"Oh, no, I found a company in Arkansas that's been making synthetic crystals for the government. Most of my sources stopped making commercial crystals from quartz long ago. Now they "grow" crystals through a lab process that combines heat, water, and, uh, a few more carefully selected ingredients. Then, they put it all under enormous pressure for a controlled period of time. I've seen it done. In fact, I visited the production facility to make sure my crystal had the precise piezoelectric qualities needed to keep a frequency stable . . ."

"I'm sorry, what kind of pie?"

"Forget the pie. We just need a crystal that will hold the frequency stable at 8.1 Hertz. We have that crystal right here—a reliable steady as she goes 8.1 Hertz."

"Okay, okay—let's say you make this experiment work. How can you be sure that someone who passes through an open portal can return?"

"You've already asked that. I can't—but I'm working on it. I've been working on a way to reverse polarity of the experiment, if needed, to bring me back."

"And who's going to be standing by to perform such a task?"

"You, my dearest friend. You."

She casually tapped my left shoulder and my right shoulder each time she uttered "you," then, with her index finger, she softly traced my face from ear to chin.

I suppressed a shiver. This woman was killing me. I drew a deep breath and refocused.

"Wait a second; wait just one second. I don't think you should bet your life on my participation."

"I'm not worried about you," she said, taking my hand in hers. Our eyes met, locked, and then, unmoving, we stared, unblinking, into the two souls behind those eyes. "I *know* you *will* be there for me. And when I come back, I'll be congratulating you on the Pulitzer Prize you won for writing an exclusive story about my experiment."

Neither of us had noticed the waiter standing next to our booth until he cleared his throat. Adele waved him off with a quick flip of her hand, and he quickly disappeared into the kitchen. She leaned towards me, her eyes scanning the room. "I better take that crystal for safe keeping."

I guess we're back in the real world.

"I'm happy to put it in your hand. Feels warm to the touch right now." I kissed her open palm and quickly replaced the kiss with the little match box. "What would cause it to be so warm?"

"You'll find out, my pretty," she said, mimicking the Wicked Witch of the West as she slid out of the booth. "Meet me at dawn at the north face of the Khufu pyramid. We'll need to get started early in order to beat the heat of the day and the hordes of tourists that'll be right behind us."

"I'm assuming one of those ley lines runs through the pyramid?"

She smiled, waved her hand and turned for the door. "Of course, and it runs through the King's Chamber. Are you sure you only received a C in physics?"

Khufu Was Never Here

The sun had barely kissed the top of the Giza pyramid when we arrived at its base the next morning.

"See that hole in the north entrance? That's where we're going." Adele pointed to a spot about fifty feet up the side of Khufu's pyramid. "It's been the fastest route to the King's Chamber since it was discovered back in the Middle Ages."

I tried to hide it, but I was out of breath by the time we reached the entrance. As my eyes adjusted to what little ambient light greeted us, I realized we faced an inclined walkway to the King's Chamber. "How far do we have to climb?"

"It's the Grand Gallery, James, and it's only about 150 feet. If you're worried about the incline, it's only 26 degrees."

"I guess that's better than 45 degrees." Every wall seemed closer and closer the farther we climbed up the Grand Gallery. *I wonder if this would be a good time to tell her that I'm a bit claustrophobic.*

"I hope you're not claustrophobic," Adele said.

"Well, now that you mention it . . .." I wondered if she could read my mind, too.

"Get over it, dude. Watch your step. Look, here's the crystal. Hold it tight, and if you feel anything, let me know at once, and don't shout."

I put the crystal in my vest pocket and gave Adele a kind-of-wan smile. "I guess it'll help me focus on something other than the stale air in here and the clammy humidity."

Adele gave a barely audible chuckle and shook her head. "I was here a couple of months ago and used my multimeter to measure the frequency in the chamber. It never varied from 8.1 Hertz even though I measured it daily over a three-week period. That's precisely the kind of stability that is essential to my experiment. Now, let's see what happens when we take the crystal into the chamber."

I took three steps forward. The walls did seem a bit close in here.

Three more steps. My cheeks flushed and beads of sweat gathered on my upper lip.

Two steps now. *Tinges of nausea . . . creeping up my throat. Focus, James. Focus.*

One step more. *A crushing feeling in my chest. A systemic burning all over. WHAT IS GOING ON?*

"Eeeyeow!" I grabbed the crystal in my pocket and jerked my hand out so fast the crystal went flying across the gallery, hit the wall about six feet away, and bounced back toward Adele who snatched it out of the air.

"I told you not to shout. Was it hot?"

"Yes, how could you possibly tell?" I gave her an eyes-wide open sarcastic glare.

I think it gave me a blister—and she asks, 'was it hot?'

"You are now an official scientist, James Maloney. You've confirmed it."

"Confirmed what?"

"That 8.1 Hertz is, indeed, the resonant frequency of the King's Chamber, and the closer you get to the King's Chamber while carrying an 8.1 Hertz crystal, the more the magnetic energy of the Chamber excites the crystal."

"Excites?"

"Yes. You know—causes it to vibrate. It's simple. The crystal stabilizes the energy while simultaneously allowing Earth's magnetic field to increase its strength as it searches for an avenue to escape the chamber. And that energy *must* escape the chamber. If the energy is allowed to escape this energy vortex, I *might* be able to harness the naturally occurring magnetic power of Earth and amplify that energy long enough to open at least one portal that *might* lead us to other worlds—and time."

"Do you realize you used the word 'might' twice in that sentence."

"I know, I know. I still have a lot of work to do before I leave."

"Leave? You're not really planning to experiment with this yourself, are you?"

"Maybe."

"Good grief."

"And you *are* going to help me."

I wanted to say 'no' but I also wanted to spend more time with Adele. With one eyebrow raised, I gave a non-committal, "Okay, I'll try to keep up."

"As Yoda once said, 'Do or do not. There is no try.' Look, I've been to the few points around the globe where the most powerful natural energy forces have been discovered. We'll probably have to connect at least three of these portals in order to create enough energy to transport me to another dimension. But who knows?"

"All right, but why not this one energy vortex? I'm not thrilled with the idea of connecting more than one. You did say Earth's energy is strongest right here in Khufu's pyramid?"

"James, if one crystal could do the job, you'd already be on the other side of the universe—or maybe a parallel dimension—since the only crystal we have was in your pocket as the strength of Giza's magnetic field coalesced around it today."

"Good grief, Adele—"

"Good grief yourself, James. Have you never put your life on the line for science?"

"I was in Iraq for the first and second battles of Fallujah in 2004. I know what risk looks like. You take a calculated risk every time you step onto a battlefield. But this risk, the one you are asking me to take, is risk in its most foolhardy and profound state. It's almost certain to result in someone losing."

"I'll try to make sure it isn't you, and I absolve you of any blame should it be me, okay?"

"No, not okay. I don't want anything to happen to you either."

Adele paused a moment, and turning slightly in my direction, she gave me an endearing little smile that seemed to reveal for the first time a mutual attraction.

"Why James, I didn't realize—tell you what—if I sense we have stepped too far with this experiment, I'll stop. I won't take any further risk. Okay?"

With that, she actually planted the softest most affectionate kiss I ever felt on my two lips.

I couldn't speak. Hell, I was barely able to breathe.

"Now, let's get back to work. This project is going to take careful experimentation as well as a bit of imagination and . . . can you hear me?"

I nodded my head.

"The crystal will stabilize each site individually," she continued, "but we'll need to find a way to connect them all and increase each site's energy. That's no small task. Earth's magnetic field can vary widely, from about 30 micro-teslas to as high as 60 micro-teslas. Harnessing that much power is the easy part; measuring and controlling it will be the challenge. That's why I packed my gaussmeter for this trip. You brought yours along, didn't you?"

"What? No. I don't even know what a, uh, gaussmeter is."

"Let me try again. Consider this: Earth, spinning on its axis, uses its iron core to generate electric currents that form its magnetic field. And a gaussmeter is used to measure the strength of the magnetic field. Every power company uses its own version of a gaussmeter to measure the electro-magnetic field under its high voltage transmission lines."

"I know that people don't want to live too close to those power lines. Now, I know why. Are you listening?" Adele had a faraway look in her eyes, a look I'd never seen before.

"No, I'm thinking. Listen to me. We'll need at least two sites that can be joined in multiplying their power at 8.1 Hertz, but most likely, three sites. I'm going to call my Arkansas crystal makers tomorrow and ask them to make five more."

"Two at each location? That's six. You're certain? Six?"

"Not certain, but that's my best scientific guess. That's the imagination part of the experiment—watch your step." With that warning, we began a careful descent down the steep inclined path of the Gallery to the blinding light of the plateau below.

"So, Adele, do you have a way to connect more than one vortex site to another?"

"Not yet, but I've been working with engineers back in the states to design a linear magnetic coupler—a very strong one, capable of handling the high power and high temperatures we expect. I believe a linear magnetic coupler offers the best chance of success. When the engineers asked me to describe the environment in which the coupler will be working, I described it as 'unknown,' and fortunately, they asked no more questions. Those nerds probably thought I was working for the CIA. And that's okay. We don't need a lot of inquiring eyes following this experiment."

As we reached the North Entrance to the pyramid, Adele's phone buzzed, alerting her to the receipt of an urgent text message. She scanned the message for only a second before whispering loudly, "Holy smoke! It works. It actually works."

"What works?" I took out a pen and began to write down every word. *This could be a major step forward in the experiment.*

"In my most recent discussion with the nerds, we agreed to use two permanent cobalt magnets in each coupler, each capable of handling

1,000 degrees centigrade, and each magnet capable of being independently aligned with separate coordinates. I just texted approval to manufacture six. Don't ask how much they cost. Two will be delivered to Giza and another pair will be sent to a friend of mine at Avebury in the southwest corner of England."

"Are we going to Avebury stone circle?"

"No, Stonehenge, just a few miles from Avebury."

"How long must we wait?"

"Two will arrive here next week. We'll need to spend some time near Khufu's energy field to align one with Stonehenge and the second with Magnetic North. My theory is that the experiment cannot be completed until we are able to tap the magnetic energy of Earth at the poles. And this is key: the magnets must be aligned precisely or we're likely to get unwanted variations in energy strength."

"Where is Nikola Tesla when you need him?"

Adele didn't crack a smile. I'll have to work on her sense of humor.

A week later, we placed two couplers at Giza with the help of one of the local guides who gladly accepted our generous bribe and led us to the perfect spot in the King's Chamber. With the aid of GPS coordinates for Stonehenge and Magnetic North, Adele carefully placed the 8.1 Hertz crystal next to the couplers sitting behind two large stones between the King's Chamber and the Gallery.

"I hope no one comes near this spot with anything magnetic in their pockets," I joked. Adele didn't smile. "Seriously, Adele, do you think anyone will disturb this spot while we're gone?"

"No, it's inconspicuous and close enough to the resonant frequency of the King's Chamber to do the job perfectly for us."

"The manufacturer will hold the third coupler pair for shipment to a 'to be determined' location . . . if needed."

"You sound like you have already selected a third energy vortex, yes?"

"Maybe."

Stonehenge

Adele's Avebury friend, Dr. Jen Mottrom, an astronomer and scientist, arranged for us to have "special VIP access" at Stonehenge in early August. But when Dr. Mottrom was told what we planned to do, she recommended that we avoid disturbing the ground within the stone circle or in the rolling hills nearby.

She didn't throw water on the whole idea, but the abject disappointment on our faces must have been obvious. "I'm aware the magnetic field on this plain is already quite strong," Dr. Mottrom said. "Surely, your coupler doesn't have to be in the center of the circle. I know a place in the nearby woods where you can place your device and secure it without anyone asking unnecessary questions."

"We'll make it work," Adele assured her. "I read a report that sunspot numbers will be particularly high on August 6. Layers of the ionosphere will be atypically thicker with negative ions the night of August 6.

"Why is this important?" I asked.

"In that condition, electromagnetic signals will be reflected back to

Earth with a minimal loss in signal strength. This will make it easier to bounce a signal around the globe from one vortex coupler to another."

On the selected date, we entered the nearby woods and dug a shallow hole just big enough to hold the two couplers. We also made sure to give ourselves a clear view of Stonehenge. Again, Adele was careful to use precise coordinates to connect the Stonehenge coupler with its twin at Giza, and the second, to Magnetic North.

We didn't have to wait long. At dusk, several rather foreboding clouds appeared on the horizon. *Could it be that the magnetic couplers have already begun to have an effect?*

Although no meteorologist in the area had predicted hail, white pellets the size of marbles began to dot the landscape until the hills around the stone monument were covered with a whiteness only seen here in mid-winter. The air, warm a few minutes ago, was utterly chilling.

These clouds did not just float in; they arrived already in a turbulent, restive state.

Thunder, with its intensity constantly ratcheting up, followed lightning's brilliant spider legs across the horizon, and contributed an ominous presence to an already disquieting scene. Something—or somebody—was angry and wanted us to know it.

As we watched from the woods, six roe deer appeared on the opposite side of the circle of stones. Three of them seemed drawn to the center of the circle. The deer never looked back at their three friends who were nervously turning 360-degree circles and pawing the ground. Clearly, they were more than a little apprehensive about joining our adventure.

The deer in the center of the circle, heads down, never looked up until an audible low frequency hum began to vibrate the air. Soon, it was the only sound possible for any human to hear—or feel. A few seconds later, the three deer froze in their tracks. Their skin began to swell; something beneath their skin began to move, creating undulating ripples until the skin of each was tautly stretched. In the next instant, the bloated grotesque deer fell dead where they stood a moment before—their eyes bulging, nostrils flared, mouths wide open with teeth bared as if in a silent scream of pain.

Ignoring the hail, we raced to the circle, uncertain of what we would find. The skin of each deer was so tight to the touch I thought it might burst at any moment.

"These poor animals are telling us that we're definitely increasing energy strength with each new vortex connected," Adele said. "I'm reminded of what would happen to humans if caught in space without their spacesuits. In the vacuum of space, blood will boil, or more correctly turn to gases—cold and full of gas bubbles."

"But, Adele, I want to point out that these deer have not been to space."

"That's what you say, but I'm not sure you can say that definitively. One thing I do know: we have work to do if we are going to increase the generated energy we need for the success of this project. And we're not there yet."

"Okay, where to?"

"I have already aligned the other half of the Stonehenge coupler to connect with the one place where all of your questions will be answered: Lake Titicaca."

"Peru?"

"Of course. And to Aramu Muru, an ancient Incan site. Locals swear it's a spiritual 'gateway to the stars.' If we're lucky, it'll be our gateway, too."

Flatland

Three flights later, we were on the last leg of a twenty-hour journey from England. My physical exhaustion was nearing its limit when the pilot announced we would be delayed an additional thirty minutes due to a storm near the airport.

"On my first trip here," Adele said, "my gaussmeter went crazy and kept rising the closer I got to the source of the energy—the portal. The electro-magnetic field registered more than 20,000 volts per meter when I approached the portal."

"Is that a lot?"

"Well, a typical microwave oven emits about 14 volts per meter, and a computer screen emits about 10 volts per meter."

"In other words, you're telling me to expect a lot of exposure to radiation at the portal?"

"Correct—possibly more than a lot. But only briefly. No lasting damage, at least I hope not."

The flight attendant interrupted to inform us that the thirty-minute delay was now forty-five minutes.

"Adele, where did you get this obsession with other dimensions? How can you be so convinced that there are more than three? I remember hearing something about eleven dimensions, usually from someone who had enjoyed too many shots of rye."

"Einstein's theory of relativity already proved there are at least two more to be explored—time and space."

The flight attendant filled my mug, she said, for a final time.

"James, did you ever read the book, *Flatland*, by Edwin Abbott?"

"No, I've never heard of it."

"Very few have. *Flatland* was published in 1884. It's full of satirical stories written specifically for England's Victorian society. Abbott was a mathematician who believed in higher dimensions. In *Flatland*, he used his mathematical skills to create a fictitious country named Lineland, a two-dimensional world that existed only on a flat sheet of paper. Mathematical symbols are the main characters in the story, and they live only on or in the paper. They had no power to rise above the sheet of paper or sink below it. Therefore, they had no concept of other dimensions until one day, the main character, Mr. Point, moved to the end of the paper and fell off the end. He discovered for the first time a three-dimensional world of height, breadth, and depth, and his perception of the universe was forever changed."

"Wait—and that's why you believe time and space should be defined as higher dimensions to our three-dimensional existence?

"Of course. Why should we limit ourselves to only three dimensions? If there are three, why not the possibility that there are six or nine— or more? Do we have no better perception of our existence than that little guy, Mr. Point, on a flat sheet of paper?"

At that moment, the plane touched down and screeched to a sudden stop on a much too short runway. We taxied to an off ramp and stopped with engines idling but still no explanation from the crew.

"While we're waiting, Adele, a couple of questions will help fill in some gaps in my story. Back in the states, you decided to skip the sites of other power vortices like Crater Lake and Mount Shasta. You must have learned something from coupling Giza to Stonehenge that pointed you to Lake Titicaca for the next coupling."

"Indeed, our little experiment at those two sites proved one spectacular thing: the coupling of high energy vortices around the world, while holding the resonant frequency of each site at 8.1 Hertz, is no small task. Therefore, the closer we can start with 8.1 Hertz, the better. My experience taught me that many energy hotspots don't have stable frequencies. Sometimes the frequencies I measured varied widely. The last thing I want is to come face-to-face with an enormous amount of electro-magnetic energy completely out of resonance with our oscillators at Giza and Stonehenge."

"Whatever you say, doctor."

"Well, we can't have a standing wave ratio greater than 1:1."

"Whatever you say, doctor. Standing what?"

"Oh, forget it, James. If my theory is correct, we only need a third and final 8.1 Hertz vortex connection. That's all you need to know."

"Well, tell me one more thing. I wanna' know why you never told me about your first visit to Titicaca. Your comment a moment ago was the first I've heard. Something happened, didn't it?"

Her tight-lipped expression told me she didn't want to talk about it. "It must have been something awful?"

A long silent pause was followed by a weak, almost inaudible, "Yes."

Give her time, James. There must be more.

"Well . . . you know how much I love dogs. Two years ago, I came to this lake on the autumnal equinox with Patches, my little red terrier."

"I heard that he died last year. Wait—do you mean he . . ."

"No, I didn't put him in the portal. It was worse than that."

"What could have been . . ."

"It was Diego, a little chihuahua, the pet of my guide, Eduardo."

"Good grief—how . . ."

"As Eduardo and I approached the portal, Diego—that antsy little puppy—sprang from Eduardo's grasp and leapt toward the opening.

Before Diego touched the ground, something smacked his snout and sent him tumbling backward. Stunned, he got up on all fours and began wobbling toward the portal. I reached for him, but was too late. His head entered the magnetic field just as full power coalesced around the portal. Poor fellow, his head was captured by the energy field; the rest of his body was left behind."

"Oh, my God!" Over and over, I repeated the words that were stuck in my throat as if on a recorded loop. "Oh. My. God." Finally, I sat back in my seat with a deep sigh. My body felt heavy in the seat.

Finally, the flight attendant's voice brought me back to reality.

"Ladies and gentlemen, welcome to Inca Manco Capac International airport." The flight attendant's cheery announcement was a welcome interruption. "We'll be at the gate in about one minute. Please check around you to be sure you have all of your belongings."

Passengers hardly spoke to each other as they stood, waiting for the doors to open. In the silence, I could think of nothing except the enormous risk Adele was about to take.

I guess I was taking the risk, too—the same risk I accepted back at Giza. As a reporter, I was all in; as a lovesick fool, I—didn't like—it.

A sixty-minute drive east brought us to our hotel overlooking Lake Titicaca. Quick "good nights" put us in separate rooms for the night. Not what I was hoping, and she sensed it.

"I'd invite you in, but you'll need a good night's sleep," Adele said, adding as she quietly closed her door, "Tomorrow, the Autumnal Equinox, is D-Day for us."

With Adele, it was always tomorrow. Would her "tomorrow" ever become tonight?

Morning arrived with a distinct chill in the air, Adele stood close to me as we gazed out over the lake to catch the sunrise she had talked about the day before. I took advantage of the moment to stand behind her and put my arms around her waist.

She didn't pull away, which was a good sign. And the view was fantastic.

The spectacular view held us in rapt fascination—and left me a little breathless. Of course, the rarified air of 12,000 feet may have contributed to my difficulty breathing. I prefer to believe it was the combined beauty of the crystalline lake and natural beauty of the person standing next to me.

"The portal is sacred to locals, but so is the lake," Adele said. "It's truly a spiritual site. Legend has it there's a gold disc at the bottom of the lake. It's said to be made of translucent, transmuted gold and, like the portal at Amaru Muru, the disc has the power to transport the bearer to other dimensions. No one will ever know, of course, because the disc and its resting place, the Monastery of Seven Rays, as it's known, disappeared beneath these waters ages ago."

"How large is this gold disc?"

"Very large and heavy. Enough to require two hands to hold it."

"An ancient Holy Grail?"

Adele pointed to a small spot on the side of the mountain, and said, "Grail? Forget the disc. *There* is your Holy Grail."

I saw only a large rectangular shaped cavity cut in the side of a large mountain of granite, less than a mile from us. The edges of the cavity were so sharp they could have been cut by a laser. From a distance, the cavity appeared to be more than six feet tall, three feet wide, and I'd guess, about twelve inches deep, maybe fourteen.

The rock reflected the sun's rays in an eerie efflorescent range of colors that seemed unsettled about their role in this rapidly evolving scene. Kaleidoscopic waves of color unfolded before us, blooming with the radiance of an eternal fountain of light.

"And there's your Gate of the Gods," Adele said.

"Where? I don't see a gate, a door, or an opening of any kind. Just a smooth indention in the rock."

"Call it what you will, James. Tonight, you and I will open that portal, or to be more precise, Earth's magnetic field will open the portal for us."

Tesla was Right

At dusk, Adele installed one of two linear magnetic couplers under a large rock a short distance from the portal and aligned it with Stonehenge. The second, she aligned with Magnetic North.

"I hope we're not generating too much energy with this final coupler," Adele said. "We will definitely be tapping into the Earth's magnetic field, but we have no idea how much power will be brought to this portal."

"You once said that 'all science is an experiment, and every failure brings you one step closer to success by eliminating another possible solution.' Something like that, right?"

"Actually, it may not be as risky as I first thought. Professor Tesla was obsessed with the number 3 and its multiples, 6 and 9. He thought the universe was governed by those numbers. What have you and I done with his numbers? Well, let's see: we've connected 3 vortex sites with a total of 6 magnetic couplers; the number 3 when squared equals 9; the last coupler was installed in the 9th month of the year; and the number .9 squared equals 8.1, the resonant frequency of Earth."

"Okay, that last one is a bit of a stretch, isn't it?"

"I'm acknowledging the risk and trying to tell you we'll be fine if we embrace Tesla's view of science experimentation. Now, let's go for a multiplier with a little injection locking."

"Injection—what?"

"Injection locking. That's what we've been doing each time we align one coupler with another at 8.1 Hertz. When an oscillator operating at one frequency—like our first oscillator at the pyramid—is captured by a second oscillator—like the one we planted at Stonehenge, both couplers will oscillate together at the frequency of the first—completely in sync."

"And the third?"

"This third site plays a critical role in our success. It must persuade Earth's magnetic field to oscillate precisely with all three couplers. The entire experiment is, well—I won't use the word 'dangerous'—but be aware that completing the entire loop by connecting this third site to Magnetic North may produce results no one, including me, can predict. Remember the roe deer at Stonehenge? Are you still in?"

"Yes—well, maybe. What's the probability that this whole thing burns us to a crisp?"

Her response was lost beneath an increasingly deep and unsettling low frequency sound.

O-ummmmmm.

The low frequency vibrations were punishing my ears.

O-ummmmmm . . . **mmmmmm** . . . **mmmmmm** . . .

Darkest clouds I'd ever seen. Some force, an invisible force, pushing them upwards, not towards us but upward.

BLAM! A jagged bolt of lightning struck the top of Amaru Muru, and the exploding thunder that followed delivered a concussive force to my body that nearly knocked me off my feet.

O-ummmmmm . . . **mmmmmm** . . . **mmmmmm** . . . **mmmmmm**.

The constant pulsations had my internal organs vibrating in sympathetic rhythm. I glanced down to see my chest moving in sync with the vibrations. The thunder was jarring, but the vibration was palpable and seemed to take control of my breathing.

"That sound is definitely coming from the ground," I shouted in Adele's direction. "This is not something spiritual, Adele. This is something else entirely, isn't it?"

At first, she ignored my question.

"Why not both—spiritual and physical phenomena," she shouted back. A crooked but satisfied smile crept up the side of her face.

I swear, the sand is melting!

Wind, whipping about my ears, was screaming like a crazed howler monkey, its intensity increasing until it became a strained screech as if being stretched in multiple directions simultaneously.

Smoke was rising from the sand everywhere.

"Holy mother of pearl, Adele, was I the only person willing to subject myself to this experiment?"

Some one—or some *thing*—touched my shoulder, then in quick succession, my head, my knee, my foot. Each touch felt like the cold possessive touch of death, a touch with no escape. Then—nothing.

"What the hell was that!" I dismissed it as sensory overload—the result of my heightened imagination.

Lightning was coming from every direction, jumping from cloud to cloud, fiercely snapping with each flash. Most of the strikes seemed drawn toward the magnetic allure of Amaru Muru.

"Lightning is a gift from the gods," Adele said, as she made the sign of the cross on her chest. "Tesla understood the potential in harnessing lightning's power. He understood the potential waiting for us."

"Tesla understood what?" I had to rely on lip reading, as my ears had become desensitized.

"Never mind, James. Yes, you *are* the only one I asked. When we were in physics class together, you described experiments better than anyone else. I need you to have a clear head to record and publish everything you're seeing in case something goes wrong, or uh, not as planned."

"Wait—what? 'Goes wrong? Not as planned?'"

"No more questions. Stand over there." She pointed to a spot about thirty yards away. As I walked toward the spot, Adele grabbed my shirt, put the gaussmeter in my hands and shouted, "Keep this gaussmeter close to you, and let me know if there is any movement. Any movement at all."

"This is nuts." *She can't hear me.* "ADELE! THIS. IS. NUTS." My mouth was moving. I was shouting, but I could not hear one word.

A thousand looms slamming their shuttles back and forth at sixty miles an hour and a fleet of jet fighters taking off simultaneously could not raise the decibel level any higher. The air shook with fierce vibrations. Barely able to stand upright, I wrapped my arms around the corner of a large red boulder and placed a vice-grip hold on it that required all the physical strength I could muster.

Images of my life fanned through my brain like a thousand flashcards, stopping for an abrupt moment to reveal the detail of my mother's face . . . and Adele's . . . before continuing into a world I did not recognize.

Somehow, I made ten mammoth strides before turning. "Adele! Adele!" I shouted again and again, but she had disappeared into a crackling mist that had slipped down the mountainside while I was struggling to walk thirty yards.

Mist doesn't crackle. I think the sound is coming from my lungs. Jesus, this is not good. Lungs are not supposed to crackle. What's happening? Is Adele in that mist?

I ran toward the mist but froze when a familiar hand touched mine. Adele was next to me, hair standing straight up, each strand snapping as if electrically charged.

"I've got to go," she said, firmly. "If I don't return in three days, press the button here." Adele pointed to a red button on the top of a device she'd never shown me.

"How does it work? What am I supposed to do?"

"Don't worry, I built this device just for you. Do as I say."

I picked up enough to understand, "Three days…push red button."

"It will reverse the polarity of this entire experiment, and if it works, if the power has not dissipated altogether by then, you'll see me again."

I picked up only "…you'll see me again."

No time for clarification. In three days, push red button.

"Wait! Adele? The needle on your gaussmeter just pegged against its highest reading!"

"James! Tesla was right! Are you still with me?"

"YES! I'LL NEVER LEAVE YOU!"

Vice grip fingers pinched my arm. As she stepped into the large cavity, she released my arm. "JAMES! I LOV. . ."

An enormous snap of static electricity cut off her last words . . . and she disappeared.

A minute ago, the cavity had been glowing a sunburn red. Now, it was the color of charcoal, steaming with a hellish scarlet glow around every edge. Horrified, I literally felt the blood drain from my face. Beneath my feet, the sand had become a creamy, liquid substance, gripping the soles of my boots like quicksand, only tighter. I couldn't raise my feet; I couldn't move at all.

Out of the corner of my eye, a grey shadow appeared, then disappeared just as quickly, spiraling into the blackness of the portal.

"Adele, is that you? Come back, Adele! Come back! I need you! Don't . . .

A thick mist embraced the entire mountaintop, and the air, saturated with the sulfuric aftermath of nearby lightning strikes, was almost impossible to breathe. Around me, everything was out of focus.

Finally, my face began to cool and images near me came slowly into focus. My eyes kept replaying images that had been seared on their retinas, images now begging my brain to decipher, to make sense of all they had seen.

And then—silence.

Deafening silence.

Shaking and struggling to create a little warmth, I rubbed my arms vigorously. The stillness of the night was my only companion. Stars above, my only light. The chill on my skin gave way to a pervasive fear that my world had changed utterly and irreparably before my eyes.

Three Days Later

I waited three days as Adele instructed and spent each lonely morning watching the sun rise over Lake Titicaca, praying in vain for Adele to come back. The one person who ever held my heart in her hands was gone. I'd trade that Pulitzer she promised just to see her one more time.

At dusk on the third day, I went back to the portal, followed Adele's instructions, pressed the red button, and reflexively yelled, "Reverse polarity!"

I forgot Adele's gaussmeter but soon discovered I didn't need one. When my wristwatch became too hot to touch, I jerked it off and threw it to the ground. Surely, the watch had sent a message that I had just achieved peak magnetic energy for the portal.

Supercharged with negative ions, the air felt the same as it often did back home after several lightning strikes, only this air seemed alive with energy. It could have been my imagination, but it seemed easier to breathe.

My heart was racing.

From the darkness of the portal a figure began to materialize. *Those long legs can only belong to one person.* As more of the image was revealed I realized the person was only wearing a cape of peacock feathers.

I couldn't take a complete breath—only shallow gasps.

The rectangular scar on her right thigh appeared even deeper than the first time I saw it but confirmed what my eyes were seeing, and my brain was trying to comprehend. It definitely was Adele Abramson. Her hair, a luminous shade of blonde and longer than I remembered—*can it grow that much in three days*—sported traces of regal red and . . . blocked my view. I couldn't see her face. But in her

39

hands, she held a golden disc.

A gust of wind blew her gorgeous curls to one side. What little breath I had been holding escaped with an urgent gasp, and my knees buckled, refusing to support me any longer. My hands covered my face to prevent me from seeing what my brain refused to acknowledge.

I have not seen this. Surely, I have not. Surely, some sort of transient floater is keeping me from focusing the image properly.

But there was nothing out of focus. It was Adele Abramson all right, her body a voluptuous vision as always, but her face—her face was the face of Diego, her guide's chihuahua, who disappeared on her first visit to Titicaca two years ago.

"Adele? Is that . . . you? Adele!"

The only sound was the whining and whimpering sound a puppy makes when it feels helpless, anxious, afraid.

I slumped to the ground, my eyes shut tight, not wanting to see again. A chilling unease swept over me, much like the unease I felt that day at Giza when I agreed to be involved in this damned experiment. And now I am totally and completely devoid of heart and soul. I feel nothing but a clammy chill.

From the lake, an Andean Coot called for its mate with a sad nocturnal chirp.

And I was alone—again.

CROSSROADS

Granulated Sugar, Please

I come for the coffee, not to make trouble.

No one would dare cause trouble in The Last Drop café, the one coffee shop in Mclean where one can enjoy a powerful cup of unblended Sumatra with a thick shot of well-pulled espresso. A Red Eye, as it is known by its many fans, offers a smooth, full-bodied flavor that delights the tongue on the way down, and leaves an after taste guaranteed to keep one in a good mood the rest of the day.

Sunny, owner of The Last Drop, knows my order will be the same every day. If she sees me coming, she'll have it ready and waiting for me on the counter before I open the door. One of her Red Eyes usually provides enough caffeine to see me safely to lunch.

Many a business meeting takes place inside the dimly lit café or outside on the patio, weather permitting. I've used the café for such many times.

Monday

The regulars are already here today.[1] One of them is the lady who settles into her seat every morning against the wall, powers up her computer, and begins writing a few more pages in her Civil War *magnum opus*. At least, that's what she tells anyone who asks. Whatever she's writing, she's been at it for more than a dozen years. Her head, always down, alternates from her computer screen to her spiral bound notebook. Her pen, constantly in motion, races to keep up with her thoughts. It's fascinating to watch, but I have long wondered who is going to type the manuscript from her tiny handwritten text. And, for heaven's sakes, why can't she finish? Margaret Mitchell only needed three years to write *Gone With the Wind*.

---

[1] [All characters are fictitious but are based on the lives of actual customers who regularly visit Greenberry's coffee shop, McLean, Virginia. Any similarity to any person, living or dead, is strictly coincidental.]

"The Office"

In the rear, near the restroom, three retired government employees enjoy sipping coffee every morning as they prepare to solve the world's problems. All they'll need for that task is half a day, every day. Wives are told "I'm going to 'the office'" as they depart each morning for The Last Drop café. One spouse, it has been reported, was happy to see her husband depart for The Last Drop. The story goes, when she learned of her husband's retirement plans, she told him, "It's fine for you to retire, dear, but I want you out of the house by eight every morning and don't come back until after three o'clock in the afternoon." And so, all three arrive at "the office" at exactly half past eight every day. Truth be known, I can't think of a better place for serious conversations about the world's problems. For this group, there are always several left on the table to consider "tomorrow."

One gentleman, a retired Marine, makes the forty mile trek every day from his residence in Occoquan. Another comes from Leesburg where he labored for the FAA during a twenty-year career as an air traffic controller for Dulles International Airport. Now retired, he works part-time for the Federal Emergency Management Agency where he is tasked with maintaining FEMA's emergency communications towers secreted down a long dirt drive, behind a barn, near the woods, and deep below ground between McLean and Leesburg. So well hidden are they that any local who happens by would not detect their presence even if he walked directly over them. As my retired friend explained to me, the antennas are kept underground to protect them from the effects of a nuclear blast— should one ever occur—over Washington, DC. Periodically, the 60-foot towers are "exercised" to confirm their operational status. Each tower can rise to its maximum height in less than sixty seconds.

I almost forgot; a special security clearance is required just to witness this remarkable process. If a national emergency should be declared by the President, a Pentagon command is all that's needed to release the full array of towers and antennas into the air.

The third gentleman retired some years ago from the CIA where he was involved in covert operations for twenty-five years. Although he's not allowed to talk about it, he was responsible for smuggling one of America's covert agents out of the former Soviet Union as the Cold War was heating up. They were forced to take a circuitous route through three American embassies in as many countries before they were able to catch a plane to the United States. That's all he would tell me.

Korean Bible Study Group

And every Monday at 10 a.m. sharp, four middle-aged Korean ladies come in with Bibles in hand. They order coffee and quickly claim the middle table by the side window. I've never heard them speak anything but Korean. At least one of them gives me a suspicious glance as if they disapprove of my presence, but they never speak to me. I'm sure they don't know I'm fluent in Korean.

Crossroads of America

To be sure, there are also ordinary people who pass through here each day, usually in a hurry to continue their busy schedules. One lady rushed by me the other day, fully engrossed in her cell phone conversation, and all I heard was, "Well, *my* life coach talks to me every day. He has the answers to all of my problems."

I wanted to ask her, "Just what is a life coach anyway?"

Well . . . to say the clientele is an eclectic bunch would be a gross understatement. Other regulars include a patent attorney, a psychiatrist, a priest, a rabbi, and one follower of a doctrine that seems to change frequently.

Political Pundits

Well known political pundits and campaign advisers are likely to drop in at any hour of the day. Most are regulars from the cable news networks and represent the full range of cable personalities. Although well off the beaten path for reporters, the little café is a favorite of at least one columnist from *The Washington Post*. Even good writers need a caffeine jolt to get them started most mornings.

Yesterday, when a talk show host from Fox News showed up, I gave him a slightly jaundiced eye. Sunny touched my arm and said, "If they'll pay for it, I'll sell a cup of my best brew to anyone who drops in—conservative, progressive, or indifferent." I think she meant "independent." Oh, well.

A true Cafecito

In the midst of all this, I try to steer a steady, even boring, course. But once in a while, I feel adventuresome and dare to try something other than a Red Eye. Last week, I even tried one of those new-fangled Nitro brews. Not a good idea. Too weak.

After I said "no" to a Nitro, Sunny asked me if I had ever tasted a true Cafecito, a drink common in Cuba. When I shook my head, she offered to prepare one for me "on the house." I *never* turn down such offers.

"It's too strong for most of my customers," she said, as she reached for the espresso beans, "because it requires a strong espresso mixed with granulated sugar. Even many coffee addicts consider it too strong and too bitter. For them, I mix the espresso with brown sugar," she said, as she poured a thick foam of granulated sugar over the espresso.

"Why not brown sugar?" I asked.

"Brown sugar contains molasses and molasses makes the drink sweet and buttery. You wouldn't like it. It would be too sweet. For you, I'll definitely use only granulated sugar. Anyone like you who's been a caffeine addict for more than fifty years can handle it."

I didn't argue. "That IS a fact Sunny, fifty-five years to be exact, but uh . . . just how much espresso is involved?" I wondered if I should reconsider my decision.

"The equivalent of three shots," she said. "But don't worry, I think you'll find it smooth and, um, uplifting."

Igor's Table

Before I could change my mind, she pointed to a table in the corner of the room. "That gentleman over there ordered one, too. You've probably met Igor. He comes in every other Tuesday for a short meeting with one of his associates. I'll bring your drink over when it's ready. I'm sure Igor won't mind if you share his table."

I didn't know Igor, but she was right about one thing. The gentleman at the table was all too happy to oblige. He stood when I approached, extended his hand, and said, "I'm Igor; have a seat."

As I pulled out a chair, the four Korean ladies closed their Bibles, reached out to hold hands and bowed their heads. A prayer, I suppose, but why did they switch to praying in Cantonese?

Conversation at the table hosting members of "the office" klatch suddenly stopped. The retired Marine tapped his ear as if adjusting a hearing aid. Funny, he never before seemed hard of hearing.

At that moment, Sunny arrived and placed an ornate porcelain cup with gold trim before me, not the usual full-size mug I was expecting. A layer of granulated sugar over the espresso appeared to have been caramelized under a brûlée torch. Whatever she used, the result was a golden foamy crown sitting atop the entire concoction. One sip convinced me that the granulated sugar was indeed essential to cutting the bitter taste of espresso.

"I see you've met Igor," Sunny said, smiling as they exchanged knowing nods of familiarity. Turning to me, she instructed with a Mother Superior air, "You *must* drink it here; you *must not* drink this one while driving."

Igor swallowed a chuckle as he watched a neophyte step timidly into a new coffee world. A few sips more had this coffee veteran on a true caffeine high, a delicious high, by the way. And Sunny was right. There would be no driving while drinking this one.

Igor took a sip of his Cafecito. "I am very pleased you will be joining the team on our next assignment," Igor said." Your reputation precedes you."

He sounds Russian, but English is too perfect. At first, I thought he was asking me to join an effort to rid the world of Russian sponsored disinformation that vexes the West and floods social media platforms. Actually, it is not uncommon for me to be asked about my knowledge of computer programming. Everyone, it seems, is searching for the originators of such mal-content on the internet.

It's great to have someone with your skills with us," Igor said. "The rest of the team is pre-positioned offshore in the Baltic."

"Wait—I think you've mistaken me for . . ."

"You ordered a Cafecito with brown sugar, didn't you?" Igor smiled a broad toothy smile.

"No, granulated sugar," I corrected.

The toothy smile disappeared and was replaced by an eyes-wide-open frozen stare.

The retired Marine pushed his chair back, and as other members of "the office" watched, he walked toward us. As many times as I've been in here, we've never met. This will be a good time for a handshake.

From across the room, the Marine called out, "Igor! What brings you to these parts?"

Igor glanced at me, then the Marine. Suddenly, both had the shocked realization that Igor should not have been talking with me.

Without another word, Igor got up and quietly walked out of the café—and never looked back. The Marine, just as quietly slipped back into his chair near the restroom table with the other members of "the office"—and he never looked back at me.

My mind was racing. What is going on? I should leave, too. I've been around long enough to know there is a time to come and a time to go, and it takes a smart man to know when his time to go has come.

I headed for the door. "And my time to go has definitely come," I said, not to anyone in particular. The door slammed behind me.

"Rats! I left half of my Cafecito back there."

Three days later, the Washington Post carried a front-page story about a surprise raid by America's Seal Team Six on a warehouse in the outskirts of St. Petersburg, Russia. The team escaped with a dozen captured private contractors and, before they left, members of the team remotely placed corrupting malware on President Putin's personal computer. Well before dawn, their job done, the entire team returned safely to the aircraft carrier USS Carl Vinson.

According to the Post story, "The present location of Seal Team Six is 'undisclosed.'"

Yes, I remain a daily customer at The Last Drop café, and to this day, when I order a Cafecito, I always ask the barista to make it with granulated sugar. I would *never* consider a substitute—especially **not** brown sugar.

COCOON

Still, They Bring Flowers

A caterpillar, in the course of its metamorphosis from pupa to butterfly, weaves a cocoon to surround itself safely until it is mature enough to spread its new wings and fly away. What would happen inside the cocoon if the caterpillar ceased to mature, its metamorphic journey halted by some unseen force? There is little doubt that its protective shell would continue to harden, sealing the caterpillar's fate. The butterfly that could have been would have no chance to develop and the caterpillar would sleep—forever. I think about that caterpillar nearly every time I have occasion to return to my deep South home.

 From the courthouse square in my South Georgia hometown of Quitman, the city limits are slightly more than a mile in every direction, its land area consisting of little more than four square miles. Not very large, to be sure, but large enough to hold the entire diversity of opinion within it—which is to say, there isn't much diversity of opinion in Quitman on any serious subject. Frankly, that seems to have been the case on almost every serious subject for as long as I can remember.

Official census records for my county in the year 1860 reveal the names of 3,067 whites. The census of 1860 also includes a numerical tabulation of slaves but no names associated with any. Slaves numbered 3,282 in the county plus two free people of color. In other words, enslaved blacks exceeded the population of whites in the county by 213.

Thus, was the difficult relationship between owners and slaves thoroughly ingrained in the DNA of most Southerners by the time the first shot of the Civil War was fired. "You have your place and I have mine; don't you forget it" was the clear message communicated to "the coloreds" over and over.

Slavery came to America like the most virulent plague, infecting the souls of all who touched it, and because there was no obvious antidote, citizens became blind witnesses to its insidious and destructive spread throughout the South. For 244 years (1619 to 1863), slavery was accepted and embraced as a necessary tool for economic growth.

It didn't help that slavery was justified to slave owners by pastors who preached a literal interpretation of Old Testament and New Testament scripture to convince willingly predisposed ears that slavery was an ordinance of God. Christians with a conscience who bought and sold slaves could assuage their guilt and their fear of violating any guiding precept from the Word of God by citing Holy Scripture, even if out of context (New Testament: Ephesians 6:5 among others). Generally, they never sought to understand the context in which the scripture was written. A pastor's interpretation was enough to continue the relationship between owner and slave. Pastors rarely helped them understand that slavery—the buying and selling of other human beings—was more than just plain wrong, it was evil.

For the Southern states, those 244 years of uninterrupted slavery that preceded secession were enough to justify every step they took to pass slavery's morally bereft nature to each succeeding generation.

Young girls brought flowers . . .

During the Civil War, most families in Brooks County suffered the loss or disability of at least one of their soldier relatives. The recording of dead and wounded was haphazard at best, particularly in the last year of the war. It has been estimated, however, that more than 200 men from Brooks County died in the war. Many families were left destitute. The collapse of the Confederate dollar helped no one get a fresh start.

Four years after the surrender of Lee's army at Appomattox Courthouse, a group of Quitman's respected Grande dames (wives, mothers and sweethearts of war veterans) established the Ladies Memorial Association. Their singular purpose was to develop the best way to memorialize those who died and honor the wounded who had returned home. The Ladies Memorial Association of

Columbus, Georgia, was the first to designate April 26 as the official date to honor all veterans of the Confederacy. Other dates were suggested, but they settled on April 26 because that was the date in 1865 when the last Confederate unit surrendered.

A small, somber group of ladies braved the late afternoon rain of Monday, April 26, 1869, for the first Brooks County recognition of Confederate Memorial Day. Each brought fresh flowers to place on the graves of their war heroes. Three young girls from the Quitman Academy stopped by later that same day to add more flowers to the graves.

The next year, more pupils from Quitman Academy accompanied their principal to the cemetery (West End Cemetery today) and each brought flowers for the soldiers' graves. They stood quietly by the graves, holding flowers reverently until invited by their principal to strew them across the graves.

A passion for an annual observance was cemented in the hearts and minds of local citizenry by 1871. A crowd of several hundred trekked from the courthouse to the cemetery that year to remember the "Defenders of the Lost Cause," as the deceased were described in the *Quitman Banner*, precursor to the *Quitman Free Press*.

The Ladies Memorial Association decided a permanent monument to the Confederate dead should be erected on the courthouse grounds. Word went out and the ladies quickly raised the $500 needed to purchase an appropriate monument. In 1879, it was unveiled in time for the April 26 celebration. The newspaper never mentioned that the monument came from "up North," in Connecticut, of all places, nor did the official program for the day list the place of its construction. Indeed, the "Yankees" at Ritter and Son of New Haven, Connecticut created monuments to Confederate dead in many communities across the eleven Confederate states.

On that special day in 1879, everyone at the courthouse unveiling agreed it was a marvelous monument. Its marble pedestal supported a granite obelisk, altogether about 16 feet in height, and weighing 9,000 pounds.

The inscription proudly declared:

OUR CONFEDERATE DEAD

ERECTED BY THE LADIES
MEMORIAL ASSOCIATION

1878

With the dedication complete, the large crowd dispersed to convene again a short time later at West End Cemetery.

Again, the youth brought garlands of flowers to place on the graves. A brass band played "Dixie," and everyone was invited to sing along.

Forgive and Forget

Was there ever any real hope that white and black citizens would join hands after the Civil War and make a smooth transition into a new era of peace and prosperity for every soul in the former Confederate states? Could 244 years of depending on slaves for the manpower to keep the Southern economy growing be so easily forgiven and forgotten? A lion would sooner lay down with a lamb, to paraphrase the prophet Isaiah.

Many are quick to argue the Lost Cause mantra: the War was never about preserving slavery; it was about an individual state's right to chart its own course, not an individual's civil rights. And indeed, many continue to believe that a state should have the right to secede from the Union if it should choose to do so. Yes, even today.

War over, but story unfinished

It is painful to review accounts of the many lynchings that took place in the fifty years following Lee's surrender in 1865. Lynchings of black citizens for real or imagined offenses were not uncommon.

A series of Brooks County lynchings in the last decade of the 19th century and early 20th century brought unwelcome notoriety in newspapers throughout the nation. December of 1894 was particularly bloody and resulted in the deaths by hanging of at least six local black men. No one was ever charged in their deaths.

In the early 20th century, Brooks County recorded eleven lynchings in a single week. But the one that garnered the most notoriety was the brutal killing of a black woman named Mary Turner. Her gruesome death by a white mob took place in May 1918.

Grand juries were sometimes convened to investigate vigilante killings. More often than not, the result was no action at all. White citizens seemed just fine with that outcome.

Still, the children brought flowers on Confederate Memorial Day. The high school marching band played "Dixie," and again, everyone sang the familiar lyrics.

Half a Day out of School

By 1953, I was in Mrs. McFarland's third grade class, and too young for a full understanding of the county's racist history. Heck, two of my good friends were children of Tobe Small, a black man whose only transportation around town was a wooden sled pulled by a mule. How I did want to ride on that sled! What do third graders know about racism?

One thing I did know: my friends and I were delighted to get half-a-day out of the classroom on April 26 to march to the West End Cemetery for the annual Confederate Memorial Day observance. And most years, it took place on a beautiful spring day. Magnolias were almost always in bloom and filled the cemetery with their majestic fragrance.

Each year, the local chapter of the United Daughters of the Confederacy awarded two silver dollars to the student from each class who wrote the best essay praising the life and exploits of a Confederate hero selected by the local UDC Essay Committee. The selection came from a carefully curated pool of wartime personalities, usually a Confederate General or Confederate political leader. I was all in for the contest but was too late to enter in 1953.

The next year, the ladies chose Confederate General John B. Gordon. I gave it a shot but didn't earn anything above "honorable mention." It was definitely a learning experience. Most important, I learned not to stray from the information provided in a biographical tri-fold prepared by the UDC. I was assured that the tri-fold contained *all* the research I would need. No silver dollars for me that year.

In 1955, they chose Confederate General Nathan Bedford Forrest as their essay subject. As Miss Paddock distributed the tri-fold to interested students in her fifth grade class, she stopped at my desk to warn me to stay within the information provided by the UDC. I suppose they didn't want me to discover that Forrest was a notorious slave trader before the war or that he became Grand Wizard of the Ku Klux Klan after the war. Clearly, there was much more to know about Lieutenant General Forrest, but those enlightenment lessons would have to wait.

Most important: two Morgan silver dollars were now mine!

As my class marched two-by-two back to our school, I asked my teacher how we were going to celebrate National Memorial Day in late May. She gave me a quizzical stare, raised an eyebrow, and said, "I don't think we do that." After a long pause, perhaps searching for something to add that would sound at least like some justification for overlooking the federal holiday, she said, "The county schools usually hold commencement exercises that weekend."

How do you escape racism when it lives in your bone marrow and courses through your veins with the equal status of red and white blood cells?

Old South Lives On

This story has been repeated over and over through the years in parts of the country where the spirit of the Old South lives on. As the 21st century opened, an organization that calls itself the Sons of Confederate Veterans was fighting attempts to erase the name of General Nathan Bedford Forrest from Tennessee buildings, parks, schools, as well as all busts, statues and tributes to him in parks, memorials, and cemeteries. Most efforts to erase the memory of Forrest were unsuccessful, that is, until 2021 when the Tennessee State Building Commission voted 5-2 to move the bust of Forrest from the capitol building to the state's history museum.

For more than 40 years the bust had been prominently displayed in the connecting corridor between the House and Senate chambers in Knoxville. And for all those years, as black members of the General Assembly walked by, they were reminded of the years of oppression their ancestors endured, and the unspoken message was clear: "White supremacy is here to stay, and don't you forget it."

In Tennessee, they bring flowers to spread across the graves of Confederate soldiers. And in Quitman, Georgia, still, they bring flowers to West End Cemetery. A few of the old folks can be heard humming Dixie as the ceremony ends.

"We have to."

Several months ago, while making a brief visit to Quitman to enjoy time with family, I ran into an old classmate who never left town after high school graduation. I wondered if he had seen many changes in all the years. He assured me there had been many and that nothing is the same as it was.

"We've had nothing *but* change," he said.

"Well," I said, "with all that change, what's the biggest problem facing the town these days?"

He grabbed me by the arm and pulled me close. "The only problems we have today are created by . . ."

Leaning even closer and lowering his voice, he whispered, "the BLACKS."

"Why are you whispering?"

"We have to be careful what we say. Political correctness, you know."

"But…"

"Don't get me wrong. Some people like to claim there is a problem with systemic racism, but I can tell you, there is no systemic racism here. We treat all just alike. We have to."

His last three words were telling.

If you lived in a small mostly rural town across the South today, you would soon discover why the gap between the races remains difficult to close. Indeed, the divide is so wide that most attempts to build a bridge across it have met with minimal success . . . although many have tried. A few perpetual optimists hold on to a flicker of hope that somewhere in that divide, the remains of a multi-cultural, multiracial potential exists. If so, it must have the "patience of Job."

In the meantime, the cocoon has turned to dust. A gust of wind has picked up its few remaining grains—once so full of hope—and spreads them like tiny seeds over the town. Some believe they will surely germinate one day . . . just not today.

Today, they bring flowers . . . still.

SIX, AT LAST

There are benefits to being number six in a succession of nine children, all of whom were born during the span of eighteen years, 1931 to 1949. Dad was the local Presbyterian pastor at the time. There were significant benefits to being a "preacher's kid," chief among them being able to gain entrance *gratis* to the Ilex Theatre on Saturday afternoons. How else was I to keep up with the latest adventures of Superman and Roy Rogers? Even better, having five siblings in front and three behind me meant parents were easily distracted from any misbehavior on my part. The oldest was going off to college in 1950 and the youngest was still in diapers. They were busy.

This young preschooler was having the time of his life, exploring every aspect of life around me.

Target Practice

Tommy Harris, a neighbor from down the street and several years my senior, received a Daisy Red Ryder Air Rifle for his birthday. The candles had hardly cooled on his cake when I went over to see his rifle in action. I was five years of age at the time—almost grown in my view. When I arrived, Tommy was firing BBs at mulberry trees across the street from his backyard. "I don't see any BBs leaving the rifle," I said, "so how can I be sure the noise I heard in the trees was caused by one of your BBs? Tommy immediately dared me to put my finger at the tip of the barrel.

I did.

My index finger had barely the time to cover the hole at the end of the barrel before he pulled the trigger.

It was later reported that everyone within six blocks heard me screaming at the top of my lungs I raced home. Mother was already standing, hands on hips, on the back porch, ominously waving a mixing bowl spoon at me long before I arrived. She spotted the BB embedded in the skin on the tip of my finger and popped it out with her fingernail. The skin was not broken. I thought I was dying. "No problem" was the way Tommy saw it, that is, until his mother took his air rifle away for two weeks. I don't think we were ever close friends after that incident.

Circle Meeting Interrupted

There was also the time my mother hosted her church circle at our house—the manse. I always looked forward to those meetings because it meant I would be left alone for at least an hour to experiment with objects I was told "not to touch." As soon as her circle convened that day, I picked up a large butcher knife from the kitchen and headed for the backyard to carve my initials on a tree. I had seen the older neighborhood kids do it and they made it look easy. As soon as the letters were outlined, the bark was supposed to peel away leaving my initials displayed perfectly. How proud mother would be, I thought, to see my initials carved so neatly. I grasped the knife with both hands and began to carve. But the bark did *not* peel away easily.

I soon discovered if one grabs the knife with both hands and pushes upward with all his strength, the bark soon would give a little. I pushed upward with all the Charles Atlas strength a five-year-old could muster. The blade suddenly slipped from under the bark, came flying upward, and before I could turn off the Atlas strength, I had stabbed myself in the middle of the forehead. Again, screaming, I ran for the back porch. Again, mother was already there; this time, a couple of the ladies, dressed in their finest, were right behind her. I think one of the ladies fainted when she saw the blood running down my face, dripping off the tip of my nose. The rest stepped back quickly to avoid getting blood on their clothes.

Mother, unfazed, whipped out a kitchen towel, wiped my face clean, and slapped a Band-Aid on the wound. "Do you think you can stay out of trouble until my circle meeting is over?" she asked. At first, I didn't say anything. When she was sure the bleeding had stopped, she disappeared quickly into the parlor. I think she did not want to hear my answer, "Probably not."

Could I help it that I had an abiding curiosity in everything. "Why does the radio work only when you plug it into the wall? Why does a bee sting? If you step on a hot coal from the fireplace, why does itmake a blister right away? And why am I blamed for every little thing that seems to go wrong around me?

A Scar? A Real Scar?

I don't think I should tell you about the small fire I started on the side of the house or the spanking I got when dad learned what happened. Mother said I would not be able to sit down for a week when he got through. That hyperbole notwithstanding, I also wondered why there had to be physical pain associated with every lesson learned? I remember dad telling all the children that "touching one of the burners on the kitchen range would burn so badly, it would leave more than a blister; you'll get a permanent scar."

A scar!? A real scar? I want one of those to show Tim and David Atkinson next door. David was my age and Tim, a year older. One morning, I watched as mother finished cooking a pot of grits. She moved the grits to a nearby burner but forgot to turn off the one she was just using. That was my chance. I placed my entire hand across the burner, palm down.

As soon as I was able to open my eyes and focus on anything in the real world, I discovered the burner had left three concentric burn circles on all five fingers. No amount of Ungentine could make the burn go away. I needed some real balm from Gilead—or from anywhere—but there was none in the house. All my siblings gathered round to see the burn and all agreed I was going to have a permanent scar. Dad, who was already a self-taught primary care physician, said, "Son, you are certain to have burn contracture when it heals." I had no idea what he was talking about. That statement ranks up there with the one he asked me that morning I wasn't feeling well and he was taking me to see a "real" doctor. "Did you have a BM this morning?" he asked when we got in the car. My computer brain analyzed in a nanosecond all the possible answers that would satisfy the question. "Yes," I finally muttered, low enough that I could change if he didn't accept it. *Okay, fine,* I thought. *I guess I'm gonna' have to become a doctor if I'm going to discuss future mishaps with him.*

The burn marks looked scary to everyone, especially me. Suddenly I was not looking forward to that permanent scar tattoo, but I needn't have worried. My very young body, accustomed to such self-abuse, immediately began to manufacture new skin, thicker and tighter than the original, but with no evidence of a serious burn. I thought I was invincible—like Superman, only without a cape. (But I still couldn't fly; I had already tried jumping over the clothesline in the backyard.)

Close Call at the Corner of Bartow and Madison

I was somewhere between five and six years of age, playing quietly by myself on the corner of Bartow and Madison streets, carefully avoiding any trouble when I heard the courthouse clock chime four times. *Fire somewhere.* That chime was the warning sound dad had described to me. Four strikes of the clock's bell meant the fire was north of the courthouse and probably not far from the manse. I stretched my body to its full height of three-feet, hoping to catch a glimpse of the firetruck. *Maybe the fire truck will come down Bartow.*

As if on cue, there it was, roaring down Bartow toward North Court Street. I watched as it crossed North Court, swung around the corner on Culpepper and disappeared down that street.

That's it? Nothing else? I don't get to see smoke?

I was about to return to the batch of Army toy soldiers "fighting" the German infantry in front of me when a driver going too fast heading north on Madison crossed Bartow. Way too fast. Just as the sedan reached the middle of the intersection, a bicycling Evans Jones, peddling as fast as he could in an attempt to catch the firetruck, also reached the middle of the intersection. The two vehicles met with a tremendous Earth-shattering "BLAM!"

There were no surveillance photos in those days, no iPhone to pull out and capture the scene, but I remember the horror of it vividly. Evans, with no time to avoid the car, had smashed into the driver's side door and was sent flying towards me. A moment later, he was lying at my feet, inches away, and screaming bloody murder. He was holding his right arm which, even to my young eyes, appeared in an unnatural state.

Mother, in the kitchen, heard the crash, the screaming, and came running. The first words from her mouth were, "What have you done now?" Not even a "Are you all right?"

I pointed to the car, the driver's side door with a deep concave indention, and the bike, nothing more than a metal pretzel, and then to Evans, whose arm was clearly broken—and frankly, I was not feeling so well myself. She finally got the picture, but I will never forget that mother suspected foul play on my part. *Had I distracted the driver, or maybe Evans? Was my reputation that bad?* I could do a lot of things in those days but getting a bike to hit the side of a 4-door sedan smack in the middle of an intersection was surely a stretch.

Home Alone

I knew my parents took little notice of me, but I was not fully aware of how little notice until the family emergency that took place when I was almost six years of age. The experience was traumatizing and even now, is recalled vividly in the way of an agonizing wish-it-would-go-away-memory. The condensed version here is all my damaged psyche is able to share.

Construction was nearing completion on the new Presbyterian Home, a residence for the elderly, that would soon open on the outskirts of Quitman. Dad, the founder, went out to the site daily to check on progress. This day, he decided to take the whole family with him. He slid behind the wheel of his 1940 Plymouth Sedan (the one with running boards for Bill and me to stand when the car was in motion, which we did each time we went swimming at Camzalea,[2] the country retreat of Dr. Simeon Sanchez, Jr, a close family friend.) Dad waved six of his children into the back seat. Mother sat up front with the youngest, Sue Ellen, in her arms. Frankie, the youngest boy, also sat up front in the middle, squeezed between his parents.

No one bothered to do the math, I guess, but only eight children were in the car. One child was missing. Even if the other siblings noticed, who was going to alert mother and dad that Roland was missing? Who, indeed? No one, that's who.

Meanwhile, back at the manse, I was having a grand time by myself. No one to bother me. Plenty of cinnamon rolls from the bakery in the kitchen—the big ones that took two hands to hold. Gradually, the sunlight faded, and the house started to darken. No one had thought to leave even one light on in the house. Shadows moved ominously from room to room as I walked about looking for any sign of the family. I heard nothing. Silence can be overwhelming at times, but this silence was more; it was deafening and terrifying.

Finally, I did what dad had taught me to do whenever there is an emergency. He probably meant the kind of emergency that involved life or death such as the house afire. "If you have an emergency like that, pick up the phone and dial zero," he said. "That'll get the operator on the line, and you can tell her to send a fire truck, the police or whatever you need."

---

[2] Combining two words, camellia and azalea, Dr. Sanchez coined a new word, Camzalea, a true portmanteau, and gave the name to his retreat.

"…whatever you need." His words echoed in my ears.

I really need my family to come home. I need somebody to fix my supper. It was already late afternoon, and I knew the three donuts remaining in the box were not going to be enough. That's what I told the operator when she came on the line.

The operator was in a central telephone office in Valdosta—about twenty miles away. If you were making a long distance call in 1949, operators were needed to connect you to the party you were trying to reach, but you had to give her a number in order for her to complete the connection, and I did not have one. I do not know how she determined that this little boy of nearly six years, was calling her from faraway Quitman, and that his entire family had left him home alone while they went for a casual tour of the nearly completed first wing of the Presbyterian Home. She knew one thing: A little boy felt he had been abandoned by his family for the rest of his life—and desperately needed someone to help—someone to prepare his supper, someone to be there RIGHT. NOW.

By some miracle, she tracked my dad to the just installed only phone at the Presbyterian Home, and in less than 10 minutes, the entire family came screeching to a halt in front of the house. I had been crying tears of fear, loss, and loneliness. But when they piled out of the car, tears of joy quickly replaced those tears of abandonment. Now, here would be someone to make my supper.

I did learn a couple of lessons that day: Tears of abandonment meant I was almost ready for first grade. And second, a boy should never be left home alone . . . at least, not until he is old enough to drive.

Fevered Teacher

I do not want to leave the reader with the impression that every day ended in disaster those first six years. At least one story from that time does have a happy ending—well, almost.

Living in the manse with eight siblings—five older than me—was like living in a full-time kindergarten. However, I missed learning basic reading skills. Fortunately for me, the best teacher in town lived across the street from the manse. Best of all she was the beautiful young Tallulah Howard. Four years my senior, Tallulah was the perfect age to tame the hyperactive young man now entering her tutelage.

Tallulah had contracted rheumatic fever the summer she turned eight and was forced to take a one-year sabbatical from elementary school. She volunteered to teach me the basics my peers were already learning in kindergarten, and mother did not hesitate to accept her generous offer. The arrangement would get me out of the house for at least half a day and she could be confident I was not getting into any serious trouble. Trouble? Hardly. I would get to spend all that time with a vision of loveliness. Learning to read came easily, but I worried that my time with Tallulah would end too soon, so, I pretended I had not become proficient in order to extend my time with her. I'll not belabor this episode, but suffice to say, I would have been the only six-year-old boy in first grade who was married—if only she had said, "yes." Of course, this episode occurred before I met my fifth-grade teacher, Miss Sally Hill, a fiery redhead, fresh out of college, who captured my attention the first day she wore those 3-inch heels to class—and she wore them *every* day.

Lawyers and Politicians

No male child of any family was ever happier to reach his sixth birthday than I. On the first day of school, dad dropped me off at the large oak on the corner of Bartow and Walker, and left me with the words, "If you can't make a hundred, make a friend." Dad pounded such aphorisms into each of us daily. "Get good grades and you can

69

be anything you want," he said, and staring straight at me, he always added, "but whatever you choose, stay away from lawyers and politicians." Of course, I did exactly the opposite. It's a miracle I lived to see my sixth birthday.

PHOTO CREDITS

PORTAL

Other Books by Roland McElroy

The Best President the Nation
Never Had - A Memoir of
Working with Sam Nunn
NON-FICTION

Seventh Messenger
FICTION

Great Scotts in Brooks County
A History of the 1st Presbyterian
Church of Quitman, Georgia
NON-FICTION

Children's Books

The Squiggle and Me
Jibicle and Cokie
The Great Mizzariddle

PORTAL

www.ingramcontent.com/pod-product-compliance
Lightning Source LLC
Chambersburg PA
CBHW060236180626
46813CB00007B/3108